To
My DEAREST
Luca,

Many thanks from
Charley ...

and Amelia Rose ♡

the Straw that Broke the Camel's Backpack

By Amelia Rose Illustrated by Matthew Maley

Archway Publishing books may be ordered through booksellers or by contacting:

Archway Publishing
1663 Liberty Drive
Bloomington, IN 47403
www.archwaypublishing.com
1-(888)-242-5904

Because of the dynamic nature of the Internet, any web addresses or links contained
in this book may have changed since publication and may no longer be valid. The views
expressed in this work are solely those of the author and do not necessarily reflect the
views of the publisher, and the publisher hereby disclaims any responsibility for them.

Any people depicted in stock imagery provided by Thinkstock are models,
and such images are being used for illustrative purposes only.
Certain stock imagery © Thinkstock.

ISBN: 978-1-4808-1274-1 (sc)
ISBN: 978-1-4808-1272-7 (hc)
ISBN: 978-1-4808-1273-4 (e)

Print information available on the last page.

Archway Publishing rev. date: 4/7/2015

"The most beautiful things in the world cannot be seen or touched, they are felt with the heart."

—Antoine de Saint-Exupéry, *The Little Prince*

Dedicated to Erika, Christian, and Alexander,
who always feel with their hearts

Charley was a very tall, very strong, very kind, and very friendly camel. He loved doing everything normal camels do: playing polo, traveling to far off places on hikes, and swimming, but more than anything, Charley loved helping everyone.

He would happily balance Zanna the Zebra's Xylophone on his back when she had a recital, or act as a hurdle for Robby the Roadrunner during gym class, or carry books for Poppy the Porcupine, Sammy the Snake, and Andy the Anteater.

Because he was so strong and kind hearted, Charley's friends always looked to him for help when they needed it.

On Charley's birthday, all his friends were at his party having a wonderful time.

Zanna gave Charley a really cool red headset, and Sammy gave him a roaring rocket blaster. Robby gave Charley a magnifying microscope, while Andy gave Charley a balloon blasting machine. Poppy gave Charley two tickets to her pet Larry the Lizard's road race.

But the present from his mother was just perfect! It was a beautiful new blue and silver backpack. Charley imagined all the things he could carry in it for everyone.

Charley's mother handed him the backpack and said, "Now, Charley, I made this backpack for you, but don't carry too much, or it may rip."

Charley smiled his great big toothy smile, and showed all his friends his beautiful new backpack. "That is the nicest backpack I have ever seen!" said Poppy the Porcupine, and Andy the Anteater, Robby the Roadrunner, Zanna the Zebra, and Sammy the Snake agreed.

The next morning, Charley saw Poppy struggling to hold her pet Larry the Lizard. "Do you need any help, Poppy?" Charley asked. "Oh, yes!" said Poppy, "Larry would love a ride in your backpack!"

Charley remembered his mother's warning, but he thought that just one small lizard would be fine. "No problem, Poppy! Climb aboard, Larry."

Just as Charley began walking again... "Charley, Charley, wait!" hollered Zanna. "Can you help me carry my Xylophone for show and tell? I'm not as careful carrying it as you always are."

Charley said, "Yes," and one by one his other friends came with their show and tell in hand asking Charley to help. Robby asked Charley to carry his tricycle, and Andy handed Charley his water balloon.

Charley pushed and shoved, and zippered his backpack until it nearly burst. But just as he was about to walk onto the bus, he heard a hiss, hiss, "Charley, please wait!" It was Sammy the snake, "Thank goodness you're here! I have been trying to get my show and tell in to school all morning, but without hands, that can be a bit difficult! Would you mind helping me with my sipping straw, just until we get to school?"

Charley looked at his bag. It was bursting at the seams, but surely there must be room for one more simple straw? "No problem, Sam! I'm happy to help."

The bus was about to leave and Charley tugged and squeezed to try to get that small sipping straw into his backpack when....

Not only had Charley's backpack broken, but his homework blew away in the wind, and his books lay torn and shredded on the desert floor.

"Hurry, hurry!" said the bus driver, "We have to leave right now or we will all be late for school!" Everyone rushed to grab their things and ran onto the school bus.

Everyone except Charley, who sat down with his beautiful but torn bag as the bus sped away.

Charley felt a hand on his shoulder. It was Grandpa Carl, "Hey, kiddo, why the long face?"

"I was trying to help everyone carry their things to school for show and tell, and I guess I overfilled my backpack. All of my friends are going to be mad at me, and I missed the school bus."

His grandfather hugged Charley and said, "I will sew up your backpack tonight. You're so nice to your friends, Charley, but you need to know your limits. They appreciate your help whenever you can give it, and they will understand if you can't always help them. Tomorrow will be a better day."

The next day was the class picnic, and Charley carried five boxes of chocolate chip cookies in his patched backpack.

When Charley's friends came to meet him at the bus stop, Charley saw that Sammy carried six boxes of strawberry strudels, Poppy carried four bags of pretzels, Robby carried ten boxes of raspberries, Zanna carried two trays of spaghetti, and Andy carried five jars of applesauce!

Charley's friend Sammy said, "We are so sorry that your backpack broke!" Poppy, Zanna, Robby, and Andy all agreed, "We won't ask you to carry everything for us again."

Charley was surprised, and very, very happy. He thought his friends would not like him if he didn't carry everything they asked him to take. Instead, Charley found out that his friends still liked him very much, and they all walked happily to school together.

Charley's teacher, Miss Muffin, came over to him and said, "I heard what happened to your backpack, Charley. Don't be so sad, because it looks like your friends made some brand new decorations for your backpack when they found out it broke."

Charley smiled his great big smile and walked to the picnic with all his friends. They laughed and played and ate together all day. Charley was the happiest camel in the world!

From that day on, Charley took his backpack on many adventures. Charley still helped his friends as best he could, but he never took on more than one camel could handle.

Charley and his friends from *The Straw That Broke The Camel's Backpack* are proud to be associated with Global Pencil Project, a non-profit organization that collects and sends pencils and school supplies to needy children around the world. Maria Vick, a writer who lived in Africa as a child, saw just how much one pencil meant to a child in Uganda. She fervently believes that education lifts children from poverty, and hopes that Global Pencil Project she founded will be able to fill the "wish lists" for teachers.

Charley will be collecting supplies at every bookstore and school we visit. If you see a sign in the window that reads, "Charley is Coming!" we will be collecting donated items for Global Pencil Project at that location.

As Maria says, "With your support, we can make a mighty difference in the world—one pencil at a time."

CPSIA information can be obtained
at www.ICGtesting.com
Printed in the USA
BVHW021808100621
609295BV00004B/11